Dedication

For Diana (Morse) Kinnersly, 1945 - 2002, who was there when the book was first dreamed of and who helped it to come true. Loved and remembered always. *SAH*

For my mother, artist and gardener. *KP*

The Mud Maid

Text copyright © 2005 Sandra Ann Horn
Illustrations copyright ©2005 Karen Popham

First published in the United Kingdom in 2005 by
The Clucket Press
220 Hill Lane
Southampton
Hants
SO15 7NR
www.Tattybogle.com

Hardcover ISBN 0-9549256-1-0
Paperback ISBN 0-9549256-0-2

135798642

Printed in China by WKT Company Ltd

The Mud Maid

Sandra Horn

Illustrated by Karen Popham

The Clucket Press

The Mud Maid watched from behind the ferns.

Will, the gardener, was planting lupins.

She winked a golden eye at him.

"Is that a fish?" said Will.

The Mud Maid laughed, "Urble! Gloop!"

"Frogs are about," said Will.

He finished planting
and trundled the wheelbarrow away.

The Mud Maid waved him goodbye.

"Feels like rain," said Will.

When Will had gone away,

the Mud Maid climbed out of the lake.

She slipped through the gardens,

in and out of the shadows,

as quiet as a fish.

She danced round the tree ferns

and into the Crystal Grotto.

She breathed the scent in the peach house and vinery.

On Flora's Green she picked a golden flower for her hair.

"All's well," sang the Mud Maid.

As the moon came up, she slipped back into the lake

with never even a splash.

In the morning, she peeped out through the ferns.

Will did not come.

"Sunday?" said the Mud Maid, but no church bells were ringing.

No-one watered the new plants, and they withered in the sun.

All day the valley was silent and still.

In the evening, when she roamed through the gardens,

the paths had not been swept.

Fallen leaves lay on the lawns. Cabbages drooped.

The Mud Maid frowned, "All a-gone?"

A cold wind scattered the fallen leaves.

On the wind came a bugle call,

and the sound of marching feet.

The Mud Maid shivered.

"Will?" she called,

but the wind blew his name away.

The Mud Maid walked slowly back to the lake.

She forgot to pick a flower for her hair.

Days went by and weeks went by. No-one came.

By the lake, the new plants shrivelled to dust.

In the gardens, fruit rotted on the trees.

No-one picked the vegetables. No-one pruned the shrubs.

Cobwebs covered the Crystal Grotto, and it sparkled no more.

Weeds grew everywhere.

Forests of sycamore seedlings blocked the paths.

"Ruin!" the Mud Maid cried.

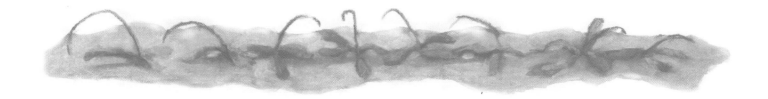

One night, a noise like thunder filled the air.

The sky was lit with angry red light.

Rooks flapped and jostled in the trees.

"War! War!" they squawked.

When the Mud Maid heard them, she wept.

She stayed under the weeds in the lake.

It was too sad out there in the gardens.

Rain softened the paths,
puddled flower beds, washed soil away.
Great storms raged.
Trees crashed down across the lake.
The Mud Maid was trapped inside
a cruel cage of twisted roots and branches.
As the years dragged slowly by,
grass grew over the fallen tree trunks.
The lake dried up.
Darkness settled deep over the valley.

Sometimes in the slow march of years,

the Mud Maid heard glass crashing,

timbers breaking, walls falling.

Then there was only silence.

The gardens slept beneath a tangled blanket,

but the Mud Maid could not sleep.

She was too frightened and too sad.

Outside, the world was changing, but she did not know it.

"How long?" she called.

No-one answered.

She had almost given up hope

when she saw a faint gleam above.

The Mud Maid blinked.

She knew she could not be dreaming;

she wasn't asleep.

Suddenly there was a cracking sound,

and a shaft of sunlight danced over her face.

The Mud Maid laughed for joy, "Urble Gloop!"

Noise and bustle filled the morning air.

A team of heavy horses pulled the cage of tangled trees away.

A blue sky opened up above.

From somewhere unseen,

cool, clear water began to flow into the lake.

The Mud Maid splashed and swam.

In the quiet of evening,

she walked through the gardens,

on new-built paths, by rebuilt walls and flower beds.

In glasshouses, shining under the moon,

she breathed in the scent of peaches and vines.

The Mud Maid clapped her hands,

"All a-new!"

Everywhere, long-hidden seeds were sprouting.

Primrose leaves pushed up through the leaf-litter.

Fern fronds uncurled.

Birds sang.

The Mud Maid danced for joy.

On Flora's Green, she picked a wreath of flowers for her hair.

The Mud Maid wandered along the Woodland Walk,
under moon-silvered trees.

A night-bird whistled a lullaby.

Moths drifted silently round her head.

"All's well," she said.

Then she lay down on a pillow of soft green moss
and smiled herself to sleep.

Other picture books by Sandra Horn

Tattybogle (Andersen Press) illustrated by Ken Brown
Rory McRory (Macdonald/Hodder) illustrated by Bee Willey
The Moon Thieves (Macdonald/Hodder) illustrated by Esther Connon
The Dandelion Wish (Dorling Kindersley) illustrated by Jason Cockcroft
The Tattybogle Tree (Hodder) illustrated by Karen Popham
The Crows' Nest (Watts) illustrated by Joseph Theobald
Nobody, Him and Me (Macmillan) illustrated by Pantelis Georgiou
Babushka (Barefoot Books) illustrated by Sophie Fatus

Other books illustrated by Karen Popham

Ellie's Growl (Frances Lincoln)
The Tattybogle Tree (Hodder)
My Ballerina Sister (Red Fox)
The Little Swan series (Red Fox):
Little Swan
Louisa's Secret
Louisa in the Wings